ROCKSTAR'S LITTLE FOR CHRISTMAS

ABDL MM Secret Relationship Romance

Jerry Hastings
Michael Levi

ISBN: 9798788520414
Imprint: Independently published

1st edition

Cover design by: Jerry Hastings & Michael Levi

CONTENTS

CHAPTER 1

Ryan

Looking at the screen, I wondered how I was going to pay for all of this. My college expenses, the electric bill, water bill, room rent, and pretty much everything else that encompassed my adult life. My hands were shaking. It was the first time I was seeing so much money I owed in my life.

Looking around me and seeing a mostly empty room, I wondered how I even managed to come here and be accepted to study at this place. I was too ambitious when I applied for it. I thought I could make everything work, that it was all going to be fine, but the opposite happened.

I loaded up my bank account app and slumped in my chair when I noticed that what I was seeing wasn't going to change just because I wanted to.

Zero. That was what was in my bank account. A big, fat zero that reminded me how poor I was.

I threw my phone away, and my heart skipped a beat when I heard the screen crack. My hands went to my head. "No, no, no," I was already saying, as I wished I was dying right now. The last thing I needed was my phone broken.

It flew across the table and fell on the floor with a loud thud. Moments later, I heard another crack. Why did everything have to go so wrong with me all the time?

I went under the table and picked up my phone, hoping that, even if it was cracked, I could ignore it. I flipped it around in my hand and I realized that that wasn't the case. The screen wasn't just cracked - it was like the cracks were everywhere.

It didn't make the phone unusable, but it was going to be a constant reminder that my life was going downhill pretty fast and that there was nothing about it I could do. I stood up, looking around and wondering how I was even going to pay the electric bill this month. They were surely going to cut it off and then my life was going to be in ruins.

I shook my head, slotting my phone back into my pocket before turning around and going back to my laptop. I exhaled a hot cloud of air, happy that at least I had this to make my life feel less like trash and more like what I wanted it to become one day.

Pressing some buttons on my laptop, I loaded up Facebook. There was this one guy from class that I liked to stalk online, and he was so handsome that he featured in plenty of my dreams.

Sleeping? It was something that just came naturally to me. I enjoyed sleeping because I didn't have to think.

Looking up, I sighed. I didn't have many certainties in life, but there was one I had. That was the fact that never again I would be a kid. Just thinking about that made my heart ache. I wanted to be a child all over again, to have my parents looking after and caring for me, and giving me everything I wanted.

I tilted my head back down and scanned the screen of the laptop. I took care of it like it was my baby, and it didn't even have a scratch. The screen wasn't like it was when I bought it, but it was in better condition than everything else I had. Even my clothes looked worn and full of holes. My classmates always gave me judging looks because of them, most likely wondering how someone as poor as me passed the entrance exam.

One day, I'm going to show them I'm better than who they think I am.

I rubbed my hands over my face, realizing that I was letting hatred take over me again. *It will not happen ever again*, I told myself before realizing how pointless that was.

My eyes blinked when I realized something different was on the screen of the computer. It was an advertisement for 'Sugar Daddies Looking for the Right Partners.'

For a moment, I didn't understand what that was about. I was no amateur in the vocabulary used in BDSM. It was already very popular around here, after all. BDSM didn't even need ads unless it was something darker or more hardcore.

Typing on the keyboard and clicking on the ad, my eyes went wide when I realized it was about something different. As soon as I was on the website that the ad led to, a pop-up message appeared.

If you're looking for the right person to pamper and make happy for the rest of their life, then this is your stop. Here we connect the right candidates to their daddies, and we try not to discriminate against anyone. If you're a Daddy looking for a Little, this is the right place for you. There are loads of Littles in here looking for men like you.

That was what the pop-up message said, and it made me feel even more confused about what was going on. I didn't know about anything behind the usage of the term 'Little.' It was alien to me and geared toward a very specific niche.

Loading up Google search, I typed the terms 'daddy,' 'little,' and some others on the bar and read everything I could about the subject. As I delved deeper into what I was reading, I felt even more surprised than I was before. From what I could see, the whole Daddy and Little thing wasn't as rare as I thought it was. There was actually a vibrant community behind it, and it wanted people like me.

But even though I had too many problems with being an adult, I would never say I was a little. Moving the pointer so that it was on the sign-up page, I began to wonder if this wasn't the opportunity I'd always been looking for. My life would be so much better if I had someone rich paying for everything I needed and wanted.

I sighed, my hands still shaking. Everything in life was a risk , but I was wondering if doing that was worth it.

I closed my eyes, took a deep breath, and clicked on 'Create Account.' All right, I was doing something I had no idea where it was going to lead to, but it was better than staying in my room thinking that my life was going to be completely ruined the next month, or the next day. All I knew was that something needed to be done.

After creating my account, the first thing I noticed was that the number of 'Daddies', who were also called 'Bigs', looking for 'Littles' like me was actually pretty huge. My pointer kept going up and down, and left and right. I didn't know the full extent of what I was diving into.

Realizing that there was no straightforward answer to that, I decided to fill up my profile. Choosing the right pictures and the right profile photo for my account were crucial decisions. It needed to be *the one* because first impressions mattered more than pretty much everything else. I was no amateur in online dating, which meant I knew just the right photos for this little operation of mine.

On top of that, writing a cool and catchy bio was just as important. No wonder I studied Marketing, I thought. I just wished it was easier to find the right connections so that I could land a good internship.

Moving the pointer to the right, I soon found what I was looking for. It was the page where all the Daddies were. There were plenty of them, and I kept scrolling up and down, realizing that it was going to take me a lot of time to find the right one.

Moments later, another thought popped up in my mind. I could show my interest in multiple Bigs at the same time. They would hopefully message me back and we would start talking about what we wanted.

I already made it pretty clear in the bio that I was looking for someone to pamper me and buy me everything I wanted. Whoever clicked on my profile and messaged me back would know that from the start. It was why I wasn't worried about disappointments.

I had little hope for this, but I was expecting to get something out of it, at least.

CHAPTER 2

John

Being a rockstar wasn't easy, especially when I had so many fools around me. I swear, it was like they kept popping out of everywhere. I was in my backstage room, the only place where I felt a little comfortable and not suffocated.

Typing away on my phone, I perked up when I heard a notification coming up. I was relieved that nobody was behind me. I didn't want anyone to find out I had an account on that dating app.

Not that there was something wrong with it, but that people would find it curious and start to ask me questions about it. I just wanted to keep that part of my life hidden for now.

It was a Little who had sent me the message and, just from looking at his profile photo, I could tell he was someone different. Even my fingers stopped typing away on the screen when I started to scrutinize every little detail about him.

I didn't think anybody would ever want to talk to me.

I didn't have a photo showing my face. I thought that nobody would ever pick me because of that. These people here all knew what the dangers of meeting someone who did that were. I was so shocked that I was already standing up quickly and pacing around in the room.

"What the…" I mumbled to myself when I realized that the guy who liked me back was as cute as a peach. He had green eyes and jet-black hair, and his cheeks bore a tone of pink that just made me feel like pinching them every day. If only he was here with me and he knew who I was and was okay with everything that defined me...

I mentioned in the bio who I was and what I was looking for. Well, except for the part that I was famous.

I'm a Daddy looking for a little. 35 years old, a successful career, and more than enough money to buy whatever you want. Don't be shy. If you're a little looking for a Big like me, I'm that person. I promise to do everything you want and to be caring and hand out punishments only every once in a while.

There'll be some rules, but I'm pretty sure someone like you won't mind them, right? Click away if that's not what you're looking for. I'm not going to show my face until we meet up in person.

That I was a publicly exposed person meant I couldn't meet up without taking some much-needed precautions. I couldn't even show my face online because I was afraid of what people would think if they found out about it. That was why I was so careful all the time.

And I was pretty sure that the guy on the other side of our chat was aware of that.

His name was Ryan, and he looked just like a normal college boy. He had unique pictures of him, and some showed him at different parties. Most of his photos were of him in his room and none were with his family, though.

I thought little that. I was still in my backstage room and happy that I finally had some free time right now. One guard would soon knock on the door to take me home, but until then, I could do everything I wanted. Knowing that brought a smile to my face. People were leaving the stadium. I finished my show not too long ago, and the place was packed then. Nothing like riding the rock wave.

Sighing, I thought that the more I looked at his photos, the more I wanted to meet the guy in person.

Ryan: Hey, I'm Ryan. How are you doing? It's so great getting to know you, Daddy!

I was giddy. Someone who knew me well would look at me and think that something was wrong with me, but it wasn't anything like that. Everything was okay with me. I was holding my phone so tightly that my knuckles were white. Ryan was genuinely interested in me. It was what I was getting from that short, first sentence he sent me.

John: Well, you don't actually know me yet, but let's talk for a little while to get to know each other. So, are you in college? I don't want to presume anything, but that's what I'm getting from your photos.

Ryan: Yeah, I am. I'm having such a hard time paying for my college bills, though. You know what it's like.

You take a loan, and another loan, and then another and many more. Before you know it, you have so many bills to pay you don't even know what to do about them.

I knew what he was talking about, but I couldn't say I had ever been in his place. My parents were very rich, as were my grandparents.

I had a very easy childhood and even though I could have gone to college, I decided not to. They wanted to disown me. It didn't happen because, in the end, they realized they were wrong.

My career pursuit was genuine, and it brought me a lot of success. Everyone in the country knew me. Or almost everyone did…

I was still pacing around in the room when Ryan answered me back after I sent him another message.

John: I know what you're talking about, but I also want you to know that it's one reason we are doing this. I want to help you however I can, even though I know we don't even know each other yet very well.

I couldn't help but imagine what it would be like to kiss him.

I wanted to feel his soft, sweet lips touching mine, and I knew he was thinking the same way.

Ryan: Right, I know. I'm excited, but you haven't shown me your face yet. We haven't talked long yet, but I'm curious about you already. And more importantly, I really need someone to look after me right now. You could be that person.

John: I'm usually busy, but we can find a nice time and spot for us to meet up. A cozy, quiet place where we would have privacy and comfort. First and foremost, I don't want you to think that I'm a criminal trying to kidnap you.

Ryan: Could you at least show me a sneak peek of your body? I promise you I won't share the photo with anybody. I'm just curious about what you look like.

Now that he said that, I realized I didn't really include that many photos on my dating profile. I put some there, but they were a little obscure. I didn't want to risk anyone finding out it was me.

Thinking that, I sat back in the chair and leaned my back on it. Breathing slowly, I opened my camera and snapped a picture of myself. I checked it out carefully to make sure it looked nice and that it was going to impress Ryan. Deciding that I was happy with it, I smiled gently and sent him the photo.

A second later, I turned off the screen of the phone because I was more anxious than I'd ever been in my life. I had no idea if he was going to look at the photo and really like me. He could end up regretting that he started this chat.

A moment later, when I was standing up, my phone buzzed, and I pressed the button on the side to turn it back on. I immediately pressed my finger on the notification icon, which took me to the dating app. I was surprised that his next message was excitingly positive.

Ryan: Wow, Daddy, you look really strong and confident, even though I can't see your face yet. Here, I'm going to snap a picture of me to show you I'm not lying about who I really am.

Since anyone can be anyone on the Internet, I know you're also a little nervous about this. I just want to show you I'm okay with your caution.

Three dots appeared on the screen until his photo finally came through. My heart was beating faster than it had ever been and even though I knew I was going to like his new photo, I was still nervous. I wouldn't say we were already in a relationship, but we were getting there.

His new photo showed him in his bed, just his face out of the comforter. He was in the same room where he had been in the other photos. Ryan was so cute and young he didn't even have a hint of stubble on his face. I could just imagine what it would be like to be sliding my hand on his cheeks before calling him my little.

I was pretty sure he was wondering the same thing, too. Our connection was strong from the very beginning. It was what I called an instantaneous relationship, or love at first sight…

CHAPTER 3

Ryan

I wasn't thinking straight when I came to this place. Nothing was wrong with it, but something was a little… odd about the guy coming to meet up with me here. Not to mention that being in such a fancy place all by myself meant people were looking at me cross-eyed.

I could almost read what they were thinking.

Who the hell allowed him in?

He's all alone, and that's creepy.

Are we sure he isn't a terrorist or an illegal alien?

Truth be told, if I were in their place, I'd be thinking the same things. But I wasn't, and so the first thing I did was to shake my head while hoping that those thoughts would leave my mind.

But that was easier said than done. I was kind of trying to make myself look as small and insignificant as possible at the table right now. I had a watch on my wrist that I kept checking out. John wasn't here yet, and I was already flaying him for that. Checking out my phone, I noticed he hadn't sent me a message yet. I didn't even know if he crashed his car and died.

If there was something I never did, it was keeping people in the dark. If someone was waiting for me and I was running late, the first thing I always did was tell them about it. But it didn't look like that was a priority for John.

Was that even his true name, though? He didn't want to show me his profile picture, didn't want to talk to me on the phone much, and said this was the only place where he could come. Something about him and journalists. I didn't understand it.

I wondered if he was someone famous. I didn't think I'd know what I'd do if that was the case. Being someone without a lot of stuff going on in my life right now, I wanted little attention on myself.

I sighed, thinking that I made a mistake by coming here. I was already standing up and looking to the side when I realized that a tall, broad-shouldered man was coming in this direction.

He stood out from the crowd and he had a bright, big aura around him. Just looking at him was already making me feel hard, and that never happened often.

Dating him meant he expected me to be his little, and even though I was kind of okay with that, I had no idea what we were actually going to be doing together. I knew it involved some age play and a lot of other things, but I didn't know how important they were going to be to him.

Standing in front of me, it took me no time to realize John was much more unique than I'd thought. I had no idea I was going to be meeting up with a rockstar in one of the fanciest restaurants in town.

He had short, blond hair, green eyes like mine, and a perfect stubble on his face. I swear, it was like he was the perfect man for me, even though I still knew so little about him.

Sitting on the chair opposite to mine, he smiled, and I noticed how bright his teeth were. It was nighttime, and he had no right to have teeth as perfect as those. They were mesmerizing me and, for a moment, it took me a while to remember I was supposed to sit down on the chair where I'd been.

Looking at me, John said, "I'm John, by the way. You were the first thing I noticed when I came in. I wouldn't have mistaken you for someone else even if I was trying to."

For a moment, I didn't even know what I was supposed to say. I realized John had certain expectations for me. If I didn't meet them, I didn't know what he would do. Certainly not anything nice, I reaffirmed.

I hope he will never find out about it...

I wasn't a little, and I lied to him about it. Nobody could blame me for having done that, though. After all, I was desperate, and I needed the money. Not to mention that I was a virgin and I couldn't keep going to all those parties - which I liked little, anyway – because all my friends always brought up how happy they were with their girlfriends.

Sitting back down on the chair, I said, "I could say the same thing. When you entered the restaurant, my eyes immediately drifted to you. I never thought I was going to date a rockstar."

John smiled. "I want to start by saying that my name really is John and that I wasn't lying about it." When he finished saying that, he looked around the place. "I love this place. I can always come here and dine out in peace. If you don't mind, I want to keep things separate. Nobody can find out about this side of me."

And I didn't want him to find out that I was a huge fan of him and his music. Bearing more importance, I didn't want him to know I was only doing this for the money. And if he were to find out that I wasn't really a little, he'd kick me out of here faster than I could beg him not to.

I certainly didn't want to find out what that would be like.

"And you can choose anything you want from the menu. I don't mind paying for anything. After all, it's why we are doing this."

And I wasn't feeling ashamed that I was going to choose the most expensive things on the menu. He was going to be my Sugar Daddy, after all. When I was old enough and had someone to look after – even though I didn't think that would ever happen – I'd be able to tell them about this. They would look at me and I think I was going crazy at the time, and they wouldn't be too wrong about that.

I was going crazy, wasn't I? I mean, how long did I think I could keep the lie up?

Licking my lips, I took my sweet time choosing what I wanted to eat. Doing that was harder than I thought. The priciest meals just didn't look that good to me. I wanted something in between.

All I knew was that my dinner with him was going to be incredible. My palms were sweaty, and I knew that after this he was going to take me to his apartment, but that was okay. I also lied to John when I said I was a virgin. I had sex once in my life. I didn't like it much, and I was still going to be pretty much a virgin when he fucked me, but still…

I was kind of hoping that our relationship would not last long. Just wanted to make a quick buck off this, pay my college bills, and then jump out of the train before it was too late. There wasn't anything wrong with that because it came with the territory.

I looked over the menu as he said, "So, are you ready to finally make your order?"

My heart was thumping in my chest. It wasn't the first time I was feeling so nervous, but it was the first time I was having a proper relationship and date with another man. There had once been a moment in my life when I thought I was straight, but it had been nothing more than a misunderstanding.

Now… It was time to figure out for how long I could keep the lie up.

CHAPTER 4

John

Ryan was so much cuter in person I thought I was seeing a mirage. I was holding his hand, and we were walking into my apartment. I closed the door to our bedroom, already taking off my jacket and wrapping him in my arms. The thing about buying him expensive stuff and showering him with paid bills was going to happen later. Right now, I just wanted to keep holding him in my arms like this.

Moments later, our lips were connected, and goosebumps were popping up all over me. They were really sweet and everything I thought they were going to be. His body was tiny when compared to mine, and I could feel him melting in my arms.

He moved his head away, looking into my eyes. Ryan was telling me a million things through the way he was gazing at me. "Daddy..." He murmured as I noticed that his voice was more high-pitched now. He was really immersing himself in age play.

I pushed him against the bed and made him flop down on it. Giggling, he tried to push me away from him, but it was fruitless. I was already on top of Ryan and peppering his neck with several kisses.

"Daddy what?" I asked with a joking tone, stopping for a moment to let him catch his breath. I wasn't going to overwhelm my sugar baby.

"Let's just stay like this for a moment," he pleaded, putting a hand on my back and moving it down until he was mere inches from finding my belt. And when he was undoing it and taking off my pants, I knew it would be a one-way trip. I'd be slotting my dick inside his rectum and fuck him so hard he would beg for more.

Of course, I couldn't really do that unless I had his okay. It was why I was being careful about this.

A moment later, I smiled and rained kisses down on his neck again. My hands took off his shirt, and I stopped for a moment to take in what my eyes were seeing. Ryan was perfect. Nothing short of perfect. He was lean, had soft skin, and his nipples were big and rosy. My hands moving up and down, I could feel a hint of abs under the skin of his belly. I didn't know if he went to the gym often, but he kept himself in shape. No denying that.

"Daddy!" He exclaimed, trying to push me off him with his arms again, but it didn't work. I was loving the way he was squirming underneath me, and I just wanted to keep this up for as long as possible. My dick was hard in my pants and I didn't know for how much longer I could keep it under control.

Lowering his pants, I reveled in the way he looked without them on. I didn't waste any time and then took off his shoes and socks as well.

The only thing impeding me right now from seeing what he was like when fully naked was his pair of dark boxer briefs, and we both knew that it was just a flimsy piece of fabric.

Roaming my hands over his body, I decided not to stop when he begged me to keep it up. Ryan didn't know it, but the way he was behaving – I could tell this was his first time. I wanted to take things slow with him, to show him that the most important thing right now was to make sure he was happy.

"I love the way you moan," I murmured, moving my hand over his thigh until I was putting my finger under his pair of briefs. Ryan didn't try to stop me when I started to lower them, which aroused me even more. He even started to help me.

I could already see the outline of his cock before, but now I could see it in full glory. It was beautiful and there was even a drop of pre-come seeping out of the slit. Ryan was so hard he was already climaxing, even though we had done nothing special yet.

"Naughty, naughty Little," I mumbled, lowering my head and starting to nibble on his earlobe. That made him squirm harder under my massive body. With my hands roaming all over his curves, I stopped for a moment to fish out a condom.

I ripped it open and took it out. Putting it on me, I smiled when I saw that my Little was already turning around so that his ass was pointing at me. He was on all fours on the bed and I knew what he was feeling. Ryan was trembling. His whole body was. I did mention we were going to have sex in our first date, so this was no surprise.

"I'm only naughty for you," Ryan said, and I couldn't help but feel that he was very much like my previous Little. But not wanting to bring back terrible memories, I pushed them out of my mind.

I grabbed him by his waist and pulled him to me. Picking up a bottle of lube and screwing it open, the next thing I did was to ready his hole for my entry. My other free hand was still roaming over his body, feeling his smooth skin, the curves that defined it, and every inch of him.

God, I loved everything about this Little.

Pushing a finger up in his asshole, I loved the way he moaned. Ryan looked over his shoulder and I nodded. It was my way of telling him that everything was going to be okay. I moved my finger deeper inside his rectum, loving how he was taking this.

His body was trembling slightly.

Every time I rubbed my finger inside him, he wanted me deeper, and that was exactly what I was giving him. A moment later, I was pushing up three fingers through his rugged hole. Seeing him so exposed, so needy for me was making me leak pre-come.

I couldn't wait for a second longer, pushing my pants down quickly and then pulling Ryan closer to me. His ass was pressed up against my cock and I loved the way his eyes were wide. He never thought I was so big.

Silly him. He should have known better.

After putting on the condom and lubing up his sphincter, I seized his hips with my hands again and pushed him closer to me. Lining up my shaft to his entrance, I started to move my hips forward slowly. I didn't want to hurt him. Everything about Ryan made me feel like protecting him at all times.

Not much longer after, I was fully inside him. I was so deep inside his sphincter that all I could see were my balls. He was warm and tight. I didn't feel like leaving him for anything right now, and I was pretty sure he was thinking the same thing.

Rolling my hips, I started to fuck him slowly while he kept begging for me to go on. I didn't feel like stopping, and so I kept on going. I had to dig my fingers into his skin, but it was okay. He didn't complain.

I picked up the pace when I realized he was already used to my size. My balls were slapping off his butt, and he was squealing. Ryan was loving every moment of this, and that was urging me to go on.

Sometime later, I came inside my condom. Holding on tightly to him, I stilled myself until nothing more was coming out. It was a little sad that I was coming inside of him with a condom on, but it was okay. Nothing about it I could do right now.

I pulled out of him a moment later. Lying down on the bed, I wrapped my arms around Ryan and pulled him to me. Hugging Ryan now just felt right. He snuggled up closer to me and deposited his head on my chest. He was light against my body.

"How are you feeling?" I asked, feeling like I was in heaven. My hand was on his back, drawing small circles on it. I just couldn't get enough of his smooth skin, and it kept me hard even though our sex was already over.

"Like I'm in heaven," Ryan responded, echoing my thoughts. I smiled, kissing his forehead. It was a pity that tomorrow morning he was going to leave, but there wasn't much I could do.

I had a show I was going to play in another country, and my agent would be pissed if he found out I was late. Not to mention that the money I was going to get from it was significant. If there was something I loved more than the person I was, it was my professional success.

For the moment, I could pretend that nothing of that needed to happen.

Time passed, and we did nothing. We just stayed where we were, listening to our breathing. His body was still quite hot, drops of sweat flowing down his curves.

"That was amazing, Daddy. I want to do it again with you," Ryan cooed, looking up. My eyes drifted to his lips, and moving my head down, I pecked at them again. Just a little, brief kiss that defined our relationship. And I was okay with calling it that. It was a relationship because we were going to be meeting up often. At least once a week.

"I know." I pecked at his lips again. "And tomorrow morning, I'll have plenty of things to show you. Gifts and other things I bought for you. I know they are the right size. You will look at them and love them at first sight."

"And you're also going to pay my college bills, right?" He asked, and I nodded. It was part of our little arrangement.

"Not just that, but you don't need to worry anymore about them. You don't have to think about money anymore. I'm going to take care of you."

And the next time he came here, which was going to take forever, I was thinking about doing a little play date with him.

I was pretty sure a little like Ryan was going to love it.

CHAPTER 5

John was holding something in his hands that was drawing my attention to it. I knew that what we were doing was going to involve this, but I didn't think it was going to happen so soon. I was in his apartment. In his bedroom, to be more precise. Everything was silent and I couldn't hear anything. Looking behind him, I remembered that this was more like a penthouse than an apartment. It had so many rooms in it and hallways and other stuff it was easy to get lost in it.

John had a diaper in his hands and a big smile on his face.

"So, what do you think about it? Isn't it cute?" He asked, padding to me. I never thought our second date was already going to involve some age play. I thought I had way more time to prepare.

Since he paid for everything, including my college bills, I decided this was something worth investing in. I readied myself for this moment as much as possible, more often than not going through nights without sleeping.

There was so much to read and learn about age play, and so much to absorb too. I knew a little about what being a Little was like, but it was still an alien thing to me.

I lowered my head and made my voice sound more high-pitched when I said, "It's really cute, Daddy! You're making me blush."

John stopped in front of me, putting one of his hands on my shoulders. He started to make small circles on it, feeling my skin under the shirt. His hand was very smooth, showing me he never had to work hard in his life. We didn't have many things in common, but that was something we had.

"You don't need to blush, Sunshine," he cooed, lowering his head and kissing my bottom lip. John was already my crush even before we met in person, and now he was driving everything I felt for him to levels much higher than I thought possible.

I wasn't just hard – I was raging hard. I couldn't keep my boner in check.

"I want you to put it on. I want to see what it looks like on you."

I knew what John wanted me to be like. Obedient, childlike, and always happy. It was with that thought in mind that I remembered to smile. Slowly and carefully, I picked up the diaper.

I thought he was going to put the diaper on me himself, but that wasn't something he wanted to do right now. John was still a couple of inches away from me, raking me with his eyes.

I wasn't feeling uncomfortable, though. When it came down to it, I felt a connection to him I couldn't deny.

Just as slowly as before, I undid my belt and let it fall to the floor. I was quite skinny, my pants falling to the floor immediately. I loved the new pants John bought for me, but he got the size wrong. It was something he needed to learn over time, as we had more dates like this one.

"Damn, you're gorgeous," John murmured, moving his hand over my body until it was almost on my ass. I stopped what I was doing for a moment to see if he was going to continue.

A moment later, when I realized he wasn't, I lowered my boxer briefs as well. I was trying to keep my boner in check before, but now it was already out and pointing at him. I wasn't ashamed of it, even though it didn't compare to his size at all.

John saw that and moved his hand down, grabbing my cock. He gave it a little squeeze and then a tug, making me moan. "This isn't fair, Daddy. I'm going to come if you keep it up."

And I wasn't lying about that. If John kept doing what he was doing, I was going to come. I would come over his pants, lose the strength of my knees, and fall into his arms. That was going to happen if he didn't-

And then he did. John took his hand off it, letting it go back to the side of his body.

"We are going to do that later, then," he said, this time shooting his hand to my balls. He squeezed them gently and gave them a little, short tug. I moaned again, my knees wobbling. I only didn't fall into his arms because I was doing everything in my power not to.

"I'm already excited about it," I said, putting a foot through the diaper, and then the other. Pulling it up, I connected the straps so that I trussed it around me. It wasn't my first time putting a diaper on, but it was the first time I was doing this while someone was looking.

And it was even more special because it was my Sugar Daddy the one watching everything from the beginning.

John put his hands under my shirt. Looking into my eyes, he asked, "Do you mind? I just think you would look a lot better without it."

I could only nod. He was going to take off my shirt, and I was going to feel even more exposed without it. I knew what this was going to lead to. He was going to have sex with me again, and I was looking forward to that so hard I was already having a pre-orgasm.

He pulled it up and over my head, tossing it to the side. It fell on his bed, as I now felt even smaller before him. John was an impressive and imposing man, and now he was showing me he was much more than that, too.

I could see the care and love he had for me in his eyes, and it was making me feel guilty. I was still lying to him about the fact I was a little. I never lied to anyone about who I was before. I always told them exactly who I was.

He raked me with his eyes again, parting his lips. I didn't need to look down to know he was hard. And to my surprise, the diaper didn't feel odd on me at all. It… actually felt good, making me feel a little safer. It was the only thing standing between me and him again.

Mickey doodles dotted the diaper, reminding me of the time when I was a kid. Suddenly, I felt like being back in that time again. I sighed, knowing it could never happen. I was an adult now, and it didn't matter how often I age played with John. I was always going to be the college guy I was.

Studying Marketing, getting stressed out with pretty much everything, and always coming here for more of this. It was what my life was all about now. Being with my Big was what made me feel less like trash. Not to mention all the little, fancy gifts he bought for me… I didn't even have to worry about buying clothes anymore.

John took a step forward, putting himself even closer to me. My head was level with his pectorals, and I could see drops of sweat rivuleting over his perfect chest. I never thought that rockstars these days worked out, but it looked like it was a thing.

He settled his hands on my shoulders, pulling me closer to him until I was feeling his feverish body against mine. He lowered them slowly, sneaking his right hand under my diaper.

It was tight, but with enough strength, he did it. I felt his fingers dancing and playing with my skin there. He closed his eyes, biting his bottom lip.

Even though I couldn't see his dick under the thick jeans he wore, I knew he was soaking his underwear with pre-come. That delicious, salty pre-come that was so much to me when I got a taste of it slightly after our first sex.

One more reason to hope he was going to fuck me tonight as well.

John had also mentioned that tomorrow he was going to take me to buy my first car. Amazing! I was already considering the model that I was going to choose, and it was going to be one of the latest. Expensive as fuck, but this burly, hairy man hugging me right now didn't mind that.

"Gosh, you're so lovely," he said, dipping his fingers into my asshole and rubbing it, turning his fingers inside of it. He'd always been inside of it before and knew everything about it.

This was his way of saying he owned me for the rest of our life together.

CHAPTER 6

John

The limo pulled up, and we got out of it. I was holding his hand, certain that the place we were going to wasn't going to rat us out. It was snowing today, and I was taking him to buy his first car. My little Sunshine was giddy and bouncing around with me. He was so thrilled he couldn't even walk like every other person.

"Whoa there," I said, advising him. "You're going to hurt yourself. Plus, I want you to behave. If you don't, there will be punishments when we come back home."

"But, Daddy!" He moaned, pouting. "I really just want to get my first car." I knew why he was so excited, but it was still interesting. I thought Ryan was into other things, but it didn't look like that was the case.

A moment later, we stepped into the car dealership. It was a large building with a lot of cars inside of it. All the walls – or almost all of them – were made of glass and concrete. Snow was falling outside, and I could even see some white dots on our vestments.

I also bought the winter jacket and pants he was wearing. To be honest, one thing I most enjoyed doing for my little one was buying him brand-new clothes. They always brought a smile to his face.

As soon as we were in the main room, his eyes drifted to one car on his right side. A moment later, he took off toward it and I had to run after him.

"Hey wait up," I shouted, getting the attention of the few people that were in the building. They looked at us with judging eyes, and I couldn't care less. I was just happy I was with Ryan and that I was making another of his dreams real.

He circled the car, sliding his hands over it. The shine in his eyes was unmistakable. This bright red coupe was the model he wanted. He was roaming his hands over it greedily, already imagining himself getting behind the steering wheel.

I didn't have to teach him how to drive. He already knew how.

I stopped where Ryan was, grabbing his hand. I loved Ryan, and he was someone truly special to me, but sometimes he needed a firm hand to keep him in check. Just didn't want to cause a scene here.

"What did I say about running off without me?" I asked, my tone firm and imposing.

Hearing it, he lowered his head and pouted. It was going to take him a while to say it, but I knew he was going to. Unless he wanted to be put in a timeout when we were back home, he had to do that.

"That you are going to punish me if I do it again," he responded, still looking down at the floor. Realizing that few people were in the car dealership building, I wasn't worried about this leaking to the public. If nobody found out about our date in that restaurant, then they weren't going to be any the wiser about this.

"That's right," I said, putting a finger on his chest. Then, I put my hand on his chin. "And if you do it again, I won't be buying you anything next time."

"Yes, Daddy," he mumbled. Seeing that I was being a little too harsh on him, I turned him so that he was facing the car he wanted to acquire. One of the latest models and the most expensive in its line. It was the first time Ryan was asking me to buy him something so fancy, and I knew it would not be the last.

When it came down to it, he just loved having a good life. I had his Facebook profile, and I had seen how he loved showing off my gifts to him.

Patting him on his back, I said, "Come on. No need to be shy. Get into the car and take it for a spin. I'm going to be with you all the way."

"Yes, thank you!" He exclaimed after one rep in the building handed us the keys. Ryan threw open the door, dove into the coupe, and spun the key. The engine roared to life and even though it didn't sound impressive, the smile on my little's face was more than enough to make me feel content with his purchase.

He drove it out of the dealership, rode through the town, and then pulled over when he said, "Oh, look. Ice cream!" He shouted so loud he even made some pedestrians throw cross-eyed looks at us. Worried, I just hoped that they weren't going to find out it was me in the passenger seat.

I put a hand on his shoulder when he opened the door.

Ryan looked at me with a raised eyebrow. "You're not going out too?" He asked.

I shook my head. "You can't go out, either. I love ice cream too, but come on – we've got lots of it in my apartment. You can eat any ice cream there and as much as you want."

"But it's not the same as hanging out with you!" He shouted again, raising his voice. I kept looking from side to side, wondering if someone was suddenly going to pull out their phone and start recording this. If there was something that always went viral on the internet, it was people throwing tantrums.

Now, I really loved my Little, and I felt a special connection to him, but what he was doing was already getting on my nerves. I stressed out so much he couldn't reveal my identity to anyone.

"It's not the same, but it's better. Up there, in my penthouse, you can do anything you want and we've got all the privacy we need there, too."

Gosh, just having this pointless argument was already a mistake. I did have some guards around, and they were in their own vehicles, but I still didn't feel safe. They always followed me wherever I went and I was pretty sure they would reveal nothing about this, even to their families, but that didn't eliminate the risk I was taking.

A single recording of this going to the public and everyone would start shitting on my career. They'd start calling me a pedophile, people would stop buying my music, and my career would be over before I even knew what was happening.

That was why I needed to take the reins of this as soon as possible.

Ryan was throwing open his mouth when I said, "No. I'm not going to keep doing this with you here. We need to leave. We need to go back to the store. I'm going to pay for your car and you will stop your little tantrum. When I go back to my penthouse, I'm going to put you in a timeout."

He opened his mouth again, but I put a finger on it. When it came down to it, even though he could be quite feisty and brave sometimes, he knew when to obey me. Ryan then shut his mouth, shaking his head.

Mumbling something, he made me wonder what it was. "Did you say something?" I asked, feeling a little distrustful of him. I mean, we already talked about this plenty of times before.

Ryan shoved the door of the car closed, turned back as tires screeched over the pavement, and raced back to the car dealership. "I'm not going to repeat myself," I affirmed, turning my eyes from side to side again. Anybody could pull out their phone and start recording this. Growing more and more paranoid as time passed, I just wanted to be out of here as soon as possible.

He sighed, showing me his disappointment in himself. "You're right."

It hurt me we were doing this, but I couldn't do anything about it. He drove us back to the car dealership, got out of the car, and after I bought it, he didn't look as excited as before about it.

I stopped in front of Ryan, putting my hands on his shoulders. "Is there something you want to tell me? I know I was harsh, but I needed to be. You know how important my career is. People can't find out about this."

"You were ashamed of me. That's not nice." He wasn't being a little anymore. Ryan wasn't a little 24 per seven, and that was understandable.

Still, I felt like we just created a rift between us that was going to be impossible to mend.

"It's nothing like that," I said, finding it difficult to get back into my Daddy self too.

All I knew was that we needed to return home. I needed a place where I didn't feel suffocated.

CHAPTER 7

I opened the door of my apartment in the penthouse, throwing my backpack onto my bed before dropping on it. I dug my head into the bedsheets and felt like ripping out my eyes. I couldn't believe I was already ruining the relationship we'd been building on this whole time.

John was pissed at me. I had the best moments of my life with him. I was in a very sugary relationship with someone willing to buy me a car worth hundreds of thousands, and I still got him pissed off when he said he couldn't go out to the street with me.

It had something to do with him wanting to keep it a secret from everyone. While I did understand where he was coming from, now I didn't even feel like taking my car for a spin anymore. And yes, it was there. Parked in front of the dormitory, glowing under the falling snowflakes.

It should be a pretty thing filling my eyes with joy, but I was feeling the opposite right now. The only thing I wanted to do now was to go back to before we acquired it.

I felt like it was tainted. After getting to know John better, I truly started to like him as a person. I thought he was the right man for me. Being for the first time in a relationship, I was still learning the ins and outs of it. He'd been showing me everything I needed to know.

I sighed, pushing myself up and looking around the room. Not having many friends meant I didn't need to keep hiding the things he bought me. I showed them off on Instagram, garnering thousands of followers these next few months. Most were probably random, fake accounts that didn't even truly follow me, but still... It was nice having them there.

My room didn't feel as empty as before.

His posters hanging from the walls, I couldn't help but feel like being in his arms again. I was putting myself in a timeout right now, sitting on the bed and wrapping my arms around my knees.

I wished I had someone to talk to about everything that happened. I wished I was in John's strong, firm arms once again and that he was kissing my forehead like all the other times we were together.

My eyes drifted to the side when I noticed something was on the nightstand. It was light blue, small, and perfect in my mouth. My hand moved above the comforter and I stopped it when I realized what I was doing.

I shouldn't be doing this. I mean, I was only pretending that I was a little to win over John's heart, right? But then, my hand kept going toward the pacifier and I... ended up grabbing it. Holding it in front of my eyes, I kept checking it out and taking in all the details it had.

I wanted to put it in my mouth. I wanted to feel like I had nothing to worry about right now.

"Don't do it," I mumbled to myself, shaking my head and hurling the pacifier away. It went all the way to the other side of the room, where it collided against the wall and fell to the floor.

Seeing that, my heart immediately skipped a beat. "Oh, no, no," I kept saying to myself, jumping off the bed and running over to the pacifier. I crouched quickly and picked it up.

I exhaled when I realized it wasn't broken. I thought it was going to have the same end as my phone. Still, I turned it around in my hand, making sure that everything was really fine with it.

Seeing that I was right, I closed my eyes and slipped the pacifier into my mouth after cleaning it with my shirt. I thought I was going to feel disgusted by it, but I was feeling the opposite. Having the pacifier in my mouth was making me feel calm and peaceful.

Even though the room was silent and it was quite depressing, I was okay right now. Certainly much better than when I entered it.

I stood up and went back to the bed, lying down on it. Fishing out my phone, I pulled up his Facebook profile. John had posted a new message, and seeing it, I read it carefully. I knew it was directed at me.

Not all things happen the way we want and that's fine. What matters is that the most important things always stick with you.

It was a short, heartfelt message that showed me he was feeling bad about the way he used those words against me. My fingers moving over the screen, I felt tempted to shoot him a reply.

What stopped me from doing that was realizing that I'd be making a mistake. Daddy never said he was angry with me, just disappointed that I raised my voice when I shouldn't have.

And either way, I should be happy he was still my boyfriend. So much so that I was already jumping out of the bed and opening the closet in my room. Now that I'd finally worn a diaper for John for the first time, I thought I needed to get more used to the feeling of having it on.

That was why I had plenty of them in the closet. Again, not having many friends meant I didn't have to try too hard to hide them from curious eyes.

Picking one up, I ripped open the plastic wrap and then put it on the bed. I pulled the sides so that it was open and ready for someone to lie on it. And even though I knew what I was doing was crazy, I decided to do it, anyway.

I took off my pants and underwear, turned around, and lied down gently on the bed. Feeling the diaper pressing against my butt cheeks was better than I thought it was going to be. Exhaling, I felt even calmer than I was before.

A thought crossed my mind. The next thing I needed right now was my Daddy lying on the bed beside me, sliding his hand over my belly. He would eventually put it under my armpits, making quick circles on the skin as he tickled me.

Grabbing the sides of the diaper, I pulled them until it was tightly secured on me. Feeling my diaper snuggly around me was already making me feel like slipping into my Little self again. And yes, I was developing that part of me, even though I thought it would never happen.

I sighed, flipping around in the bed, my pacifier in my mouth. I closed my eyes and thought of my Big while I tried to fall asleep. But even though I felt at peace, I didn't know if sleeping was going to be a possibility tonight.

I thought I could keep going on with our relationship without that thing bothering me. But then the moment he said he couldn't have ice cream with me outside, putting his career success before our relationship, I realized things were going to be more difficult than I had thought.

I picked up my phone again and pulled up his profile. I checked out his photos, one after the other, remembering what his body was like. His lips were like heaven every time he kissed me. John said nothing about a little secret of mine when we fucked for the first time. He didn't mention he knew I was a virgin. For him, that was just the cherry on top.

I wanted to feel him inside of me, but I had a rule. I couldn't do that while I was my Little self. I didn't want to feel like a pedophile. Knowing he wouldn't like that, I was already preparing for the worst.

John said that next time we would meet up in a very special place. There was this room he built for his ex-partner in his penthouse. He thought he couldn't even open it again after what happened, but I was helping him with getting over it and now he finally felt ready.

I sighed, pressing my lips more tightly on my pacifier. I could dig this. I could put it in my mouth more often, even when John didn't want me to. I had no idea if that meant I was falling further into the world of littles, but I wasn't going to struggle against it.

Moments later, I was already asleep like a baby.

CHAPTER 8

Alright, this was much better than before. I crouched, turning on the faucets. Water started to fill up the bathtub. When it was almost full, I turned them off. Using a mixture of hot and cold water, I made it feel lukewarm - and perfect for my little.

I stood up, turning so that I was facing him. "Come on, arms up," I said, and he obeyed me. Something was different about him this time. It was like he was doing this to mend what we went through that day.

I was just happy that what happened that day appeared to be behind us.

Having pulled up his shirt, I took off his pants and then his shoes and socks. My hand slid over his body accidentally, and it made me want to play with him right now. On my bed, where we could have all the comfort we needed. But even though his cock was hard and pointing at me, I wasn't going to do that.

Looking up and into his eyes, I asked, "Feeling better now? I know we went through something horrible, and I just want to make you sure you still don't hate me for it."

I kept my hands on his sides, making sure he knew he had my support no matter what happened. Hearing what I said, Ryan shook his head. "Don't worry about it. It was nothing."

I pulled up the corner of my lips. "That's what I like to hear." Turning my head to the side, I said, "Put your hand in the water and tell me what it feels like to you."

I was asking him to do that because I wanted to make sure he liked it. After he dipped his hand in the water, he said, "It's really good, Daddy. It's perfect, actually."

I was a little relieved he said that. For a moment, I thought he was going to say it was too cold or hot. But that's not what happened, and now I could proceed to do that other thing I had in mind.

Ryan dipped his feet in the water, and then his whole body. Water moved from left to right and vice versa in the bathtub. It hid most of his body, but I could still see his private parts.

I grabbed a bath sponge, squeezed some liquid bath soap on it, pressed it with my hands to create foam and bubbles, and then started to wash his body. We didn't speak for the first two minutes, but then I felt that he wanted to say something to me.

Turning his head to me, Ryan affirmed, "I'm really sorry about the way I treated you that time."

And I was hurt he felt he needed to explain that to me. This was a moment where he was supposed to immerse himself in his Little self, and not bring back bad memories.

I waved my hand in the air. "Don't worry about that. You lashed out at me, and I lashed out at you. It will never happen again."

He pulled up the corner of his lips. Even though Ryan was hard, I felt that nothing was sexual about this. I was bathing him, and this moment wasn't about anything more than that.

"Thanks, Daddy. It really means a lot to me when you say those things."

Sliding the bath sponge over his leg, I said, "Don't think about it again. All I want you to be right now is my Little."

A moment later, Ryan said, "Do you think I could watch TV until late tonight?" Hearing his question, I looked into his eyes and pondered what my answer should be.

"I'm going to think about that," I responded, finding it hard to keep my boner in check. Gosh, there was just something special about Ryan. I couldn't find the right words to describe it, but the connection I felt to him made me care about him more than I would with any other person.

"How does this feel?" I asked, willing him to change the subject of our conversation. I was brushing the bath sponge over his dick and scrotum, applying just enough pressure to make him even harder than he was.

Ryan's cheeks blushed a beautiful tone of rose, and that made me feel like kissing him harder than ever before. And not feeling like wasting any time, I did that right away.

I didn't just kiss his lips, though. I also pecked his forehead, feeling a variety of things, and they were all good.

"There. Finally feeling better now, little one?" I asked, taking the bath sponge out of the water and putting it in the cradle in the bathtub. He smiled, nodding slightly.

"Yes, I'm feeling much better now, thanks to you."

He moved his hand to the small plastic duck floating in the water. Picking it up, he put it right in front of his mouth and looked at it almost like he was trying really hard to focus on it.

"I'm thinking about making a song about you," I said, throwing that out in the wind to see what his reaction was going to be like.

He was kind of looking at me using the edge of his eyes before, but now he snapped his head so that he could see all of me.

"Really? Wow, I never thought you would. I'm already dying to listen to it."

"It's just something I need to do to make up for that ice-cream incident."

"But I thought you said we weren't supposed to talk about it anymore…"

"Don't worry. We won't. I was just… Never mind what I was

thinking. Just wanted to make sure that everything is still good between us."

"It is," he said when I grabbed his cock and gave it a stroke under the water. He moaned, sealing his lips with mine all of a sudden even though he didn't need to. That was Ryan's way of telling me everything was going to be okay from now on.

"So, how's the water now?" I asked, throwing some shampoo in his air and rubbing it. Little bubbles still coming out of the water, Ryan giggled.

"It's really great. I knew you were going to get the temperature right on your first try." He took a deep breath, looking somewhere I didn't think he was going to tell me anything about. "You're really… never going to tell anyone about us?"

Ryan was staring into my eyes, and I could tell that was a very important question to him. I sighed, realizing that he was eventually going to ask me that anyway.

"You need to realize that my career is one of the most important things in my life."

"More than me?" He asked.

I didn't feel like saying it to his face, but right now, he was still just my Sugar Baby. It hurt me having to think about it that way, but there was no other way to put it. I was just supposed to feel good about this by giving him expensive stuff.

"As I said before, I don't want to think about that." I took my hands out of his air, standing up. "And, we shouldn't even be worried about it." Sighing, I decided to change the subject of our talk. "And now please stand up so that I can dry you with the towel."

Ryan exhaled loudly, standing up. I picked up a towel, looped it around him, and then started to rub his body with it. Ryan was dry in no time, which was perfect. I couldn't wait until I was putting a diaper on him for the first time.

"I guess we better don't talk about it again." That's what Ryan said and even though it hurt me we were bringing up that subject again, I supposed I couldn't keep running away from it. "Changing the subject, I'm really looking forward to seeing what that coloring book you bought me is like."

I shook my head, blinking rapidly. "What… coloring book?" I asked, forgetting that I was in the bathroom, with my little, and that we were just supposed to be cherishing one of the most intimate moments of our lives.

Ryan smiled, cocking his head left and right quickly.

"Daddy, please don't play the fool with me. You know what I'm talking about. You said you bought it for me yesterday." He grabbed my hands, jumping out of the bathroom with me. Ryan was still naked, and I was seeing his behind as we left the bathroom. "I'm so excited about it! I know you spent a lot of time choosing it for me."

As I followed him out of the bathroom, it occurred to me that Ryan was right. There was this coloring book I bought for him yesterday, and I did spend a lot of time choosing it.

I even ordered it from someone who said he bought it in another country.

I stopped when that realization popped up in my mind. Turning to the right, I opened the closet and picked it up. My mind had been still so focused on the discussion we had I didn't remember that I was supposed to give him this gift.

Holding it out in front of me, I said, "Here, and thanks for reminding me about it. You're going to have a blast with it."

CHAPTER 9

Ryan

It wasn't fair what happened. John shouldn't really be doing what he was doing. Hiding our relationship from everyone just wasn't right. Or... Was it? I asked myself, seated in the passenger seat of his limo. I loved everything he always bought for me, but now that our relationship was developing and becoming more than the whole sugar thing, I wanted to show everyone that he was my partner and love.

He pulled up in front of my former home. The pickup truck and the other car in the driveway told me that my parents were home, just like I thought they were going to be.

The problem with meeting them was that John was doing something he wasn't supposed to. He said and stressed out how important it was to him that we kept our relationship secret. I had no idea what was going on in his mind right now. Did he think that my parents were going to be okay with our relationship?

But I supposed I needed to trust him first and foremost. My arms crossed over my chest, I felt comfort and safety in the way he was putting his hand on my thigh. I didn't come here as a Little, and the fact that I still hadn't told him about that lie was kind of beginning to eat me from the inside out.

I mean, if he ever found out about it, that I was never a Little, the first thing he would do was to kick me out of his life.

The sky overcast, snow falling to the ground, I could see blinking lights coming from the living room. My parents were in the house and getting ready for Christmas. It was going to be a very special time for me and my caretaker. I knew he was preparing something even more special than all his other gifts to make me feel pampered.

He turned his head to look at me, and I could see the strong love he felt for me. I knew that, if there was someone in this world who made me feel loved, cared for, and everything else a Little like me could ever want, it was John.

"I know how important this is for you, but this is also very important to me. I'm making an exception this time. I'm going to show them we are together and then I'll ask them to keep it hidden from everyone. I'm sure they're understandable people, like you."

It was kind of cold even inside the limo. I wore heavy, thick clothes for the winter. The only thing I wanted to do right now was to be outside, playing a snowball battle with him. But I supposed this was something we needed to get out of our system, and we needed to finish it as soon as possible.

"They're not even going to think twice before telling their friends about it. Even being out here is a risk. I know that there aren't a lot of criminals around here, but there are probably some journalists snooping around. You said you were going to buy me something even more expensive than everything you already bought. Why not do that instead now instead of wasting time here?"

And right now I just wanted to be coloring the drawings in that coloring book he bought me. And then, when darkness enveloped the city, I wanted him holding me tightly and making love to me in his penthouse. I'd wake up in the morning, look over the city from the glassed balcony, and I'd remember how lucky I was that I was now living with him.

And yes, we switched to living together now. In his penthouse. I couldn't be any happier.

"I don't think that's going to happen. I talked to them over the phone, said that I was someone different, and they told me that it was okay. They still think that they're only going to be meeting your new friend, but it's a start already."

I sighed, realizing I wasn't going to change his mind now. After all, if I were to try doing that, I knew it wouldn't work.

He opened the door, stepping out of the limo with me. My mom was already rushing to the door and throwing it open. I knew what she was going to say before she did.

"My little Ryan! I'm so happy to finally be seeing you again." And when she turned her head to look at who was accompanying me, she squealed. That was a problem with being in a relationship with someone so famous. "Wait, I can't believe you are with The Reaper! I'm such a huge fan of him."

She sped up towards us, hugging my boyfriend tightly. I snapped my head toward them, finding it unbelievable what was happening. I knew she liked him, but I didn't think she was such a huge fan. She even seemed to have forgotten about me.

"Mom!" I said, asking for her attention. After all, we came here because I needed to tell them about us. Looking over her shoulder, I noticed my dad in the door. He was leaning on it, his arms crossed over his chest.

Just looking at him was making me feel a little nervous. It wasn't that we had a terrible experience while I was still living with them, but that we didn't have anything in common. It meant that while I was growing up here, he never connected to me.

The person that most connected to him was my adopted brother. I waited a few seconds to see if he was going to show up behind my father, but that didn't happen. Maybe he wasn't even here?

My father pushed himself away from the door, stepping through the snow as he made his way toward us. "It's good to finally be seeing you again, my son." He checked John from bottom to top. "And even though I kind of suspected I knew your voice, I didn't think you were the same person. So, you're his boyfriend?"

The moment he said those words, I felt that a huge weight lifted off my shoulders. I didn't think he was just going to say it right away like that.

"Dad... I didn't think you knew about it. I mean, I was still thinking about the right time to reveal it."

He waved his hand. "Nah, this is the right time for that, and you know it."

I supposed he was right, but he was still making me feel uncomfortable about it. Shifting my weight from left to right, I said, "Well, with that out of the way, now I need to get my mother off my boyfriend."

I cracked an uncomfortable smile, hoping that I wouldn't have to be doing this. But she was still rubbing her head on John's chest, making me wonder what was really going on in her head.

I poked her shoulder and she finally snapped her head toward me, little snowflakes in her hair. Shaking her head, she blinked twice until she realized I was still here.

My mom was still the same person I knew. She hadn't changed at all since I left. They lived a good life and I didn't need their money anymore. I mean, I kind of did... Or I did a lot, but I wasn't going to admit that.

"How the hell did you two end up meeting each other? This whole thing feels so surreal. I never thought you were gay and would end up stealing the heart of the most amazing man in the world."

And she was saying that right in front of my father, who was still looking at us with kind eyes. He was the kind of man who went out hunting often, fished in the lakes and rivers nearby, and liked hanging out with his friends.

I wasn't like that. I didn't even like drinking. Before finding out that I felt a connection with the world of Littles, I just wanted to continue being someone different from the person my father was.

Now that this whole thing already started, I knew that everything was okay. I was relieved that things were taking this direction. I chuckled, thinking that few things in life were better than my mother being the person she was. Growing up, she was the person I was most connected to.

My mother and my father introduced themselves to John, who was happy to greet them. Turning so that he was facing the house, my father held up his hand. "Don't you want to come inside with us?" He asked, and the smell coming from inside it was already making me giddy.

We were going to have a nice, warm dinner with my family, and I was pretty sure it was delicious.

CHAPTER 10

John

Something was off about him, which was why I was worried. He was seated on my lap, his body feeling very small and light on mine. I wasn't going to say anything about that, though – at least for now. My mind was still immersed in the fact that I got his family's okay for our relationship.

We were in our penthouse, the blinking lights of the Christmas tree behind us dotting the TV's screen. It was Christmas and for such a special occasion, we were doing something different.

Now that I was thinking about it, it was the first time we were sharing such a special and intimate moment together. Ryan had his onesie on, the pacifier in his mouth, and was clutching a teddy bear to his chest. He liked to call him Stuffie, which was cute and just like him. I knew he was going to come up with a cool name for him.

Seated on my lap like this, he was making it hard for me not to think about ripping that onesie off him right away and penetrating him, fucking him until it wasn't Christmas anymore. But I knew that wouldn't be appropriate.

Not to mention that I could see his reflection on the floor, showing me he was almost asleep. I was happy he was feeling so comfortable. If he was so sleepy, then it meant nothing was bothering him too much. My arm wrapped around his body, I could even feel the beating of his heart and also how he kept gently rubbing his butt to my dick.

I knew he was feeling sleepy and I kept reiterating that to myself, but when he was being so naughty, punishments needed to be delivered. Still, handing out punishments on Christmas night? Something was telling me I shouldn't do that.

I smiled, happy that was the biggest worry in my mind right now.

Little Ryan finished coloring that coloring book I bought for him some time ago. So much time passed since then it was like it happened in another life. Anyway, now that we told his parents about us, part of me couldn't help but feel like telling everyone else.

Not the part about us doing the things we did behind closed doors. Perhaps I could ask my assistants to start throwing some rumors around about us. If that worked well, sharing the truth with everyone would be easy peasy. Well, perhaps not that easy, but easy enough.

"Hey, are you still awake?" I asked, rubbing a thumb over his cheek.

He perked up, not taking his pacifier out of his mouth. When we were playing, he needed to obey all the rules I specified for him, and that wasn't something he liked doing much.

I wondered why, especially after living for so long with me. To be honest, I'd always wondered about something from Ryan's past I still hadn't asked him. I didn't know if now was the appropriate time to ask him questions about that, but the thought was still in my mind, and keeping it in check was challenging.

Ryan nodded, showing me he understood what I asked, even though he was so sleepy he might as well have been sleeping when I asked him that question.

"I was wondering if you could finally tell me how it was that you found out you are a Little."

After asking him that, I took his paci out of his mouth. Now that I did that, Ryan could speak freely.

"But Daddy, I don't want to talk right now. I just went to sleep in your arms."

Him asking me that was making me wonder if I was doing the right thing by probing him about his past. I didn't want to make him feel like I was prying, even though I was.

"Well, you don't need to answer my question right now, but I'd still appreciate it if you did."

He squirmed in my arms, rubbing his head slightly against my chest. Making small circles on his torso, I wondered if he was going to answer my question or not. Maybe he was a little too sensitive about it.

Time was passing and I could see he was thinking about it. "It was a friend of mine who introduced me to it. I honestly thought it was weird at first, but then he showed me I didn't have to think about anything when I was a Little. I thought that it was fantastic and thus I couldn't go back to being my former self. Months later, I found you, and then you decided to become my Sugar Daddy. You know the rest."

So that was what happened, though I couldn't shake off the feeling his story was lacking somewhere. I mean, that was all of it? His introduction into the world of Littles was pretty straightforward and painless. It wasn't like it happened to me.

"Now that you know, it's only fair that you told how you became a Daddy. I'm overly curious about it."

"I didn't tell you about my parents, how I was raised." I took a deep breath, weighing the right words. "They thought something was wrong with me when I told them I was gay."

"You mean they thought something was wrong in your head? That must have sucked a lot. I thought they supported you."

"No, we didn't have anything in common. It wasn't as easy as it was with you and your family," I said, playing with his bottom lip for a little while until he was giggling. "And then everything went downhill when I told them that I was a Daddy looking for a Little like you. They went crazy and even attempted to hook me up with a psychologist, but of course that didn't happen, and so now here I am with you."

Little Ryan turned his head, looking at me with wide eyes. "I really thought someone as successful as you had an easier upbringing. I'm sorry things were like that."

"Hey, don't be. Life sucks like that sometimes."

Having said that, I still couldn't help but wonder about something he just finished telling me. Could it be possible that we could… Fuck. I didn't know if I could ask him that without feeling a little horrible about it.

Still, I couldn't push that nagging thought out of my mind, no matter how hard I tried.

A moment later, my little Sunshine fell asleep. I smiled, not even trying to wake him up. I was happy he was finally having sweet dreams. I didn't tell him anything about it, but tomorrow morning we were going to be opening even more gifts.

Putting him in my arms, I took him to our bedroom. Closing the curtains, I put him down on the bed and covered him with the comforter. My little sunshine looked so cute right now, his cheeks rosy like flower petals.

I noticed he was holding something I must've overlooked before. It was a small book, like a diary. Raising one of my eyebrows, I picked it up. Why the hell did he have a diary with him? I asked myself, putting some distance between us.

I didn't want to feel like something was wrong with him and our relationship.

I shouldn't be doing this.

That was the first thought popping up in my mind. And yet, I was still opening the diary and reading the first page. It mentioned something about his long, already forgotten past. When he wasn't even in college. It looked like he didn't have a good upbringing with his parents. Ryan never really connected to them.

I flipped on to the next page, reading it. Little Ryan mentioned something about the way he didn't like a certain friend he had in high school. He said that he thought he was someone he could trust, but that he ended up losing his trust. Reading that one more time, I felt like burying him in my hug.

I wondered if the diary was something he ended up forgetting about, but which he just remembered he still had. I didn't know the answer to that, thinking that all I could do was flip on to the next page, which I did.

And on this page, I noticed my name written on it. My heart was in my throat as the thought that I was breaking my promise not to invade his privacy kept coming up in my mind. I really, really shouldn't be doing this, but then I would be curious all the time – and I wasn't sure this diary was something I could ever bring up.

And so, I started to read the page where he talked about me.

John is a really nice guy, and a lot more than I thought he was. I thought that for being someone so famous, he was going to be an ass, but that's not who he is. After our first date, I'm already making it official. I'm going to become a Little. I'm going to turn into the Little he is looking for, and I'm going to milk him for all the money he has. It will be the life-turning point I've always been looking for.

Perhaps it was the honesty behind it, but those words hurt me more than I thought they would.

I never thought that Ryan had been lying about it this whole time…

CHAPTER 11

Ryan

I woke up hoping I was going to find my Daddy opening the door and coming to me with a tray of breakfast in his hands. But the room was silent and I couldn't see anyone inside it, other than me, of course. Lying in my bed, I turned my head left and right. From up here, in his penthouse, I could see pretty much everything in the city. All the buildings, houses, roads, and vehicles. The only thing I couldn't see was people walking in the streets.

Snowflakes falling from the sky, I knew this was the day after Christmas I was waiting for. We didn't have a Christmas tree in our bedroom, but we had it in the living room. We decided to do something a little simpler for this Christmas. Just one Christmas tree, a really big one, full of boxes and gifts underneath it, but no more than that. John said he wanted to make it so each gift was significant.

I could see where he was coming from with that. No point in having a perfect Christmas morning if the gifts he was going to give me weren't all meaningful.

My stomach rumbled. What I wanted right now, more than the gifts he bought me, was him lying beside me. I wanted to be in John's arms, to feel the heat of his body, and the beating of his art. Was that really something so hard to have this morning? I asked myself, realizing I was being unfair.

John could be somewhere else in the penthouse, preparing something even bigger for me. It was as I thought before. He wanted to give me everything I wanted, to make me feel pampered like the Sugar Baby I was, but he would never make it so I didn't think his gifts weren't some of the most important parts of my life.

I got out of bed and said, raising my voice, "Daddy? Where are you?"

A moment later, I was walking across the floor when the door opened. His eyes were teary and red, like something terrible had happened since he woke up in the morning.

Seeing that, I ran up to him immediately. I swung my arms around him and hugged him tightly. I had no idea what happened, but I wanted him to know he had my full support.

A moment later, I was expecting him to put his arms around me as well. But that didn't happen, which made me look up and find his troubled face. He was looking at me hurt, a tear rolling down his cheek. My heart skipped a beat. I had never seen my Daddy this way.

"What's going on?" I asked, knowing that it was the only thing I could ask right now.

"Oh, my little sunshine. I don't even know how to say it. I really, really thought you were the person I thought you were."

"What are you talking about?" I asked, refusing to push myself away from him. I wasn't going to distance myself from John as long as I felt he needed me. It was supposed to be the other way around, but it didn't matter.

After a moment of silence, when I thought he wasn't going to answer me, he put his hands on my shoulders and moved me away from him. I blinked twice, going after him right away, but he lifted one of his hands and stopped me.

"My whole life, I've always avoided confronting people when needed. This time, it's going to be different. You lied to me and you need to know that's wrong. I really thought we were building toward something special. I was even already trying to show people we are together, but now that doesn't matter anymore..."

Part of me was trying to make me hug him again, but it was obvious he didn't want me to do that. And when it came down to it, even though I didn't think he could ever hurt me, I didn't want to try him.

And so, I stayed where I was, with just my diaper on. He must have taken off my pacifier and onesie when I was sleeping. He always did those things so that my nights were comfortable.

"I still don't get why you are doing this. I don't remember doing anything wrong."

When I woke up and got out of bed, I was already in my Little mode. But now, I wasn't. I was just my normal, boring self. I couldn't be a little when John was acting like this. Tears coming out of his eyes, he was making me feel guilty about something I had already forgotten about.

My eyes lowered when he lifted his other hand. He was holding something in it, and it was a piece of my past I really thought I had forgotten about. My diary. I had no idea why I even had it with me. I must have brought it when I moved into his penthouse.

"It's my diary."

"I know it is."

"I hope you didn't read it. You said you were always going to respect my privacy."

Something on the left side of his neck twitched. It was one of his veins. I pissed him off even more than he already was.

"I read it and I discovered your secret." After a moment of silence, his eyes staring straight into mine, he was already making me feel uncomfortable. And when he said the next thing he was thinking about, I knew it was going to have the impact of a bomb. "You were never a little. You were only pretending you were."

I took a step toward him quickly, moving my hands frantically to try to make my point clearer. "It wasn't anything like that!" I said, knowing I was lying to him again. Maybe I was a compulsive liar, but that was a topic for another time. "I wasn't a Little when I met you, but…"

John cocked his head. "So, I was right. You were never a Little. Are you even a Little now, or is this all still part of the lie?" He asked, his eyes firm and determined. He was making it difficult for me to answer that question without feeling like I was an asshole.

Our relationship was going so well I had even stopped thinking about that. I stopped remembering that it started from a lie. But I was only doing that because John never wanted to tell anyone about us. And for someone so worried about that sort of thing, everyone needed to be aware of it.

And that included my parents. When I found out they were okay with it, the first thing I did was to make a new decision – that everyone was going to know about us. I knew it was going to take a lot of time, but I was okay with that.

"You were never a Little and you were only doing this for the money."

I perked up my head. Now he was approaching a matter very sensitive to me.

"I did it mostly for the money initially, yes. But you need to remember you were okay with that, too. That's what being a Sugar Daddy is all about, after all." I took a deep breath, pondering my next words. "But things have changed since then. I love you now. Just… Please stop doing this to me."

My heart was tight, tears coming out of my eyes. I had no idea if he was going to see things from my point of view, but it was the only hope I had.

"You still lied to me and you never tried to show me the truth. I'm not sure I can even trust you anymore."

"But you can trust me! I'm trying to tell you the truth. You showed me how beautiful life can be. I was missing so much this whole time."

He lifted the diary, putting it on a small table by him. "After reading your story, I don't think so. I don't know if I can even trust anything coming out of your mouth ever again. You lied so much to me."

I took a step forward. "Yes, I know I lied, but then everything became genuine. I really started to love you, and I still do. You are everything to me."

John lifted his chin slightly. He was looking down at me in disdain. "Get out. Get out of my penthouse."

His words impaled my heart. I had no idea what he was even saying. He wanted me to get out of his penthouse even though I had been living in it this whole time? Where was I even going to go?

"But I don't even have money to pay for a room anywhere. You can't just kick me out like this."

"Doing this hurts me a lot, but I don't see another way. I can't trust you anymore."

I lowered my head, realizing I wasn't going to win this. John was right. I betrayed his trust when I didn't tell him the truth. Stepping toward the door, I walked past him and headed out.

Walking down the hallway, I hoped he was going to say he was sorry and that I shouldn't go, but it didn't happen. After going through so many hallways and rooms in his penthouse, all the memories I had came back with the speed of a jet plane.

I fucked everything up again. I ruined the most perfect relationship I had. All because I never had the courage to be truthful to John. His penthouse was now silent and devoid of life. On a normal morning like all the others we had, he would be running around with me, playing together until we were both tired.

But now... All those things were absent.

I stopped in front of the elevator, pressed the button, and waited until a ding echoed. It was surreal what was happening and I felt like I wasn't in my body anymore. I actually felt like I was in the body of someone else.

The doors rolled open and I stepped into the elevator. I wasn't even taking my things with me. I knew that John was going to send someone with them to where I was going to be. I also knew that he was going to give me some money so that I could find a place to be for today and all the days that were going to come afterward.

I had no idea how I was going to survive without his presence and the support he always gave me, but that was okay. Or as okay as it could be.

I wasn't even taking Stuffie with me and that was saying a lot. He was always so important to me. I always brought him wherever I went.

I just couldn't do it. It was like not even Stuffie mattered right now.

CHAPTER 12

John

I had no idea what I was doing when I said those things to him. The moment my little Sunshine wasn't in my penthouse anymore, I was already feeling that I made a huge mistake. I gave him money, his things, and all the gifts I was going to give him, but I still felt like I didn't do the right thing.

Turning the bottle, I took a long, everlasting chug of the expensive wine in it. The liquid was warm and comforting, making me feel less like trash right now. It was the only thing impeding me from jumping over the short glass wall of the balcony and falling onto the street.

It was in the bar of my penthouse, with no one else accompanying me. The place was desolate and the only thing remotely making me some company was my guitar. It was by the wall of the bar, standing imperious. I wanted to pick it up and play a song, but I didn't even feel like getting off the stool.

My agents kept calling me and asking me what was wrong. I had to even turn off the phone so that they stopped bothering me. I didn't feel like talking to anyone right now.

This morning, I didn't take a shower when I woke up. It even took me much longer than normal to get off the bed. Without my little Sunshine by my side, cradled in my arms, I couldn't do the things I always did. Every morning, I'd run around in the house with him and we would play hide and seek.

Sometime after that, I'd even put a new diaper on him. I'd call him my little Sunshine over and over, rubbing my snot over his belly and tickling him. Ryan was a very ticklish little. Even though he said he didn't like that, the smile on his face always betrayed him.

I took another long chug of the wine, feeling a little drunk, but not too much so. I'd turned off my phone and now was thinking I shouldn't have done that. It was the only way I could connect to Ryan again. I just wanted to be putting a pacifier in his mouth – a new one, straight from France – and saying that he was the most important person in the world to me.

I thought that becoming a Sugar Daddy was what I'd always been looking for. After having terrible experiences with other Littles, in normal relationships where expectations were different, I thought I just needed something that didn't come with the same baggage. Something lighter, that involved less romance. I wanted only the good things that came with being in a relationship.

Fuck. The word 'love' kept coming up all the time in my head.

My hair was a mess. I didn't even put on new clothes this morning. And the funny thing was that someone on the outside wouldn't even suspect something was wrong with me. If I was in a show and playing my music, they'd just think I was being my normal self.

How wrong they would be.

I sighed, getting off the stool when the door to the bar room flew open. In marched one of my agents, a feisty old woman with sizzling hot, red hair and big, hipsters glasses. She strode toward me so fast she moved like a blur, shoving a finger against my chest.

"You're coming with me," she stated, staring into my eyes. "There's a surprise show coming up in town, and you need to be there."

"What?" I asked, but she was already taking me away from there and back into the limo. "But I'm not even ready. I didn't even take a shower."

She shook her head, urging the driver to take us there. He was speeding up the limo like this was the most important race of his life. Snapping my head left to right, I was more confused than anything. This sort of thing never happened before. They never took me anywhere without enough planning and preparations beforehand.

"What's going on here?" I asked and she snapped her head to me again.

"You know what it is. I'm going to mend the mess you made."

For a moment, I didn't know what she meant by that. Mulling it over, I soon concluded that I didn't even have time to find out what her reasons were. We were going into one of the biggest stadiums in the city. Seconds later, I was crossing the main door, sitting on a stool, and hairdressers and makeup specialists were preparing me for a show.

Minutes later, I walked through the curtains and stopped in my tracks when I spotted someone I thought I'd never see again. This wasn't a normal show open to the public. There was just one person on the field, and he was looking at me with tears in his eyes.

He was behind this in part, I thought. He must have talked with my agents and they must have realized I was planning on doing this all along. I'd always been thinking about doing something just as big to get his attention.

Picking up my guitar and holding it in my hands, I could only tip up my chin and reaffirm the importance of making the most of this. This was the opportunity I needed to make peace with my little Sunshine again.

Tears coming out of his eyes, I could see he was also holding Stuffie in his hands. It was his way of telling me he was a Little now and that nobody could take that away from him. And, by playing my guitar and starting a new song I was making just for him, I was saying I was giving ourselves a new chance.

This time, there were going to be no more lies and we were going to make up for all the time we lost.

RYAN'S EPILOGUE

I ran up to John and hugged him, loving the way I felt in his arms. I pressed my head tightly to his chest, just wanting to be with him for all of eternity. I had no idea this was going to be happening, that he was going to be giving me another chance.

Looking up, I could see the big smile on his face. He put his hand on my head, moving it down and up. "I made a big mistake. I hope that the song I just made for you is going to make up for that."

I pressed my arms more tightly around him. "It did. It was beautiful. Thank you for giving me another chance."

His agents were still in the same room and were looking at us, their hands clenched. Their eyes didn't lie. They were all worried it wasn't going to work, that our plan was going to be a bust.

It was them who contacted me first. At the start, I thought it was a prank or something similar, but it hadn't been. They wanted us together again and I could see why. John couldn't live without me.

He lifted his arm and moved so that he was standing by my side. With his arm draped over my shoulders, he pointed toward a spot in the room. It led to a backstage room in the stadium, where they'd applied makeup on him and chosen his attire. It didn't hide his clumsiness and morning laziness, though.

I was standing right in front of him, holding his hands.

"I came here so quickly I forgot to bring your things. I mean, you shouldn't be here without your paci. I know how important it is to you."

I chuckled, realizing that he didn't have to worry about that. My hand went into the pocket of my pants, and from there I got something. Holding it in my hands, I showed it to him.

"Do you mean this, Daddy?" I asked, taking a step toward him. "I brought it with me when your agents said we were going to be meeting."

John widened his smile, squeezing my hand a little more tightly. "So, you were the one behind this after all. It was just as I thought."

"Something like that. I just thought I should take advantage of the opportunity that was sprouting up." I leaned in closer to him, putting my head on his chest. "And now I'm here with you again and everything is fine. I'm really sorry I lied to you."

He brushed his finger over my cheek. "No need to worry about that. I'm sorry I tried to hide our relationship from everyone. It will never happen again, and tomorrow I'm going to make an announcement. I'm going to tell everyone about us."

I took a step away from him, looking up. "Are you sure? I don't want you to put your career at risk."

"I'm more than ready for that. It's the right thing to do."

I was feeling a little guilty about it when he grabbed my hand, pulling me so that I was closer to him again. He was holding me so tightly against his body I could feel the beating of his heart. It was calm like I thought it was going to be. *Like I thought it was.* He wasn't doing this because he was being forced to, but because he knew it was the right thing to do.

Looking up, I said, "Thank you. For everything you've done for me, thank you. You're the most important person to me, and I want you to know that."

And now that we were together and he was holding me like this, I was already thinking about all the good things we were going to be doing when we were back in his penthouse. He was going to put a new diaper on me, call me his little Sunshine again, and then give me gift after gift as he pampered me.

I was looking into his eyes as I realized he wanted to do just one thing right now. I was still holding my pacifier in my hands and I didn't put it into my mouth yet. I wanted John to do that for me.

John lowered his head, connecting his lips to mine. When they touched, it was like fireworks exploded in my head. I felt tingles all over my body, pressing my body against his more tightly. I just wanted to become one with the person who cared about me so much.

His lips were so sweet, so tender I didn't want to end the kiss for anything. I had to go on my tiptoes so that I could be doing this, but it was worth it. I wasn't even aware I was doing that. I'd grown used to it.

He dug his tongue into my mouth, battling against mine for possession for a few seconds. It wasn't like I could win a tongue battle against him, and I wasn't going to pretend otherwise. I just wanted to be dominated and put in a position of submission.

Our kiss was hot, needy, and very wet. My lips kept rubbing against his, and I was already beginning to feel a little out of breath.

Minutes later, which felt like hours, we stopped kissing. John moved his head away a little bit so that his eyes could take in all of me.

"I love you so much," he purred, and I could see how much that meant to him, which was immeasurable.

"I love you too." And saying that felt so right I almost fainted, such was the strength of my love.

JOHN'S EPILOGUE

I knew we were going to end up together again, but I never thought it was going to be like that. We were back in our penthouse, and I was holding him in my arms. He was seated on my lap and I was seated in my old, but comfortable chair. It rocked back and forth as I read a short story for my little prince.

He didn't have anything on other than his pacifier in his mouth and his onesie. The onesie was bright green, with cartoon doodles all over it. Disney doodles, to be more precise. They were so cute that every so often my eyes drifted down to look at them.

His pacifier was bright green too, to match the color of his onesie. Holding the book right in front of him, it featured a story I'd read not too long ago. It was called Biker's Little for Christmas, telling the story of a biker that found his eternal little while going on a trip in the mountains. It was also set on Christmas.

Christmas was well over for us now, but we could still look forward to something just as exciting. The New Year. People were already getting ready for it.

The colors in the city were changing, from mostly white to a composition of different colors. It was all getting brighter, more colorful, and dare I say it, even more exciting.

It was dark outside and I could see rounds of small snowflakes falling to the ground. From up here, I could see that the city was still covered in snow. It made me want to go out there to play with my little one, but it was cold and I could see he was almost falling asleep.

This was a new beginning for us. No more lies and pretending we weren't together for real. No more having to keep the truth hidden from other people. I already told everyone about us and even though they had no idea about our kink, everything was perfect. They didn't need to know about that, and neither did little Ryan think we needed to tell anyone about it.

I closed the book when I finished reciting the last word. I thought Ryan was going to say something about that, but he didn't. His body was light against mine and it just made me want to tuck him under a pile of covers.

I didn't say anything for the next few minutes, just waiting to see what his reaction was going to be. Even though we were standing behind a huge window, I couldn't see his face and I didn't know for sure if he was already sleeping. All I knew was that he was breathing slowly.

I kissed the back of his head gently and then stood up with him in my arms. Even though Ryan was very much an adult, he was still very light, especially when I was holding him like this.

Walking to the hallway, I stopped when he started to stir. Looking down, I thought I was going to see him opening his eyes, but he didn't. What I saw was just the cute face of someone that meant the world to me. He was sleeping like a baby, and tomorrow morning we were going to do something even more exciting than all the things we already did.

I was going to have a snowball battle with him.

I walked down the hallway and turned to the left when I reached our bedroom. Even though he had his crib, he preferred sleeping in the bed with me.

I laid him down on it, pulled up the comforter, and then walked around the bed. I took off my clothes, having nothing on more than my underwear. I pulled up the comforter, slipping myself underneath it.

I put an arm around my little one and then gently moved until my body was slightly pressing against his. I knew how important it was for Ryan to be sleeping with his pacifier in his mouth, but right now I wanted to do something else.

I looped my fingers around the handle of the pacifier and then pulled it out of his mouth. I did it slowly because I didn't want to wake him. My heart ached when he started to stir again, but then I noticed that his eyes didn't open yet.

I exhaled. I thought I was going to fuck this up.

Gently, remembering that one time he said he didn't mind it, I pressed my lips to his. They were peachy sweet. I remembered that this was one of the things he most wanted to do with me. My little prince wanted to wake up to my lips kissing him, and I was making that happen. I was always going to do everything he wanted. That was the whole point of our love. I was always happy when I was pampering him.

A moment later, his eyes were beginning to open.

He was a little groggy and it took him some time to realize that it was just me who was in front of him. "Daddy..." He murmured, putting his arm around me and pulling me to him so that we were hugging each other more tightly.

"Shhh, little one. Go back to sleep. I'm going to be with you the whole night. And tomorrow, we're going to do something exciting."

"Really?" He asked, closing his eyes again. "I can't wait..."

And I could say the same. I was fully, deeply in love with him.

The End

Thank you for reading this story! If you're looking for the first three books of the series, check them out here:

1. Rockstar's Little: ABDL MM Halloween Romance

2. Doctor's Little: ABDL MM Halloween Romance

3. Biker's Little for Christmas: ABDL MM Stuck Together MC Romance

Lastly, leave a review for this book if you liked it. It really helps us a lot!

ROCKSTAR'S LITTLE

ABDL MM Halloween Romance

Max

I was in my room, leaning over my table. In front of me, my notebook, sheets of paper, and my computer. On the other side of the room, scratches on the wall. My cat was curled up on herself, sleeping and snoring. Sweat was pooling on my forehead and I could only wonder when I was going to finish my homework.

My hand was holding a pencil, and I hated calculus. I kept wondering why we had to keep trying to solve these problems. It wasn't like I'd use them when I was working for a company, right?

A notification popped up on the screen of my computer and my hands flew to the keyboard. It was my friend, saying that he also couldn't find solutions to the problems. I smiled, knowing that was one of the few things still making me happy tonight.

It was so good to know Claude always had my back.

Me: I know, right? I also don't know the answer to problem one.

Claude: It's going to get better, I'm sure of it. You just need to believe in yourself.

Believing in myself was one of the things I thought I'd never be able to master. It was so hard. Dating? Forget that. It was impossible for someone like me to date, especially at a college that was so conservative.

It was like I could feel people judging me all the time. Eyes on me, always checking out what I was doing. I was gay and I couldn't even go to a bar without checking out the guys there. They were all my type. Well, most of them were anyway.

And I had no idea why my mind was even thinking about that sort of thing right now. I knew it was kind of impossible, but I still tried to control those thoughts. I just wanted to have one night where I didn't have to think about those things. One night when I was alone and all I had was my homework.

I looked at the screen of the computer again and noticed that my friend had gone offline. It was just like him to disappear from time to time. To be honest, that was what I should be doing right now. I should be focusing on myself and my homework.

I looked outside, happy that at least I was living in my own apartment. It was solitary, but noises were absent. I could even sleep now and I was feeling pretty sleepy.

The only thing keeping me from sleeping was my homework. Seeing all of the sheets of paper on the table, my notebook, my laptop computer, and my pencil and eraser was driving me nuts.

I took a deep breath and tried to control my thoughts. The last thing I wanted now was to fall into another spiral of depression. I had depression once and I could never have it again. I almost killed myself then.

It was thanks to my only friend that that didn't happen. And he knew that, which made me pretty sure he was going to talk to me again soon. Part of my mind was begging for him to do that.

I took another look around the room and noticed posters on the walls. I was a pretty big fan of a rock band and I was dying on the inside to go see them when they came here. It was going to happen next week. I invited my friend to go there with me and he said he was going to. I liked going with him to places, and even though he said he wasn't into the rock band much, he said he was going there with me anyway. Just to keep me company.

I sighed, worked on the homework a little more, and tried not to freak out about it. The last thing I needed now was freaking out about anything. Just wanted to remain calm and pretend I really was going to get that Economics degree.

I hated this college. Just wanted to get out of it as soon as possible and find a place that didn't despise me as much. It even had a church on campus, and I was forced to go to mass even though I didn't want to.

This whole thing was such a mess.

A notification popped up on the screen again.

Claude: Something's on TV. I think you should turn it on.

Me: And you're not even going to tell me what it is?

Claude: Not this time :)

I sighed, standing up. I was happy I didn't have to keep trying to finish that homework. And the due date? It was tomorrow morning, or maybe today. I didn't know for sure. I wasn't keeping track of time anymore. Doing that made me feel nervous and I hated that.

When I stood up, my cat cracked open her eyes. A collar was around her neck, with her name engraved on a small pin. Chill. It also had a tracker and some other things in case she disappeared.

I lived in an apartment and I'd never let her out without my permission. It was something we established when I found her. She'd been lost in an alleyway and I couldn't have let her there all by herself. Still had no idea who dumped her there, though. And I didn't think I'd ever find out.

I walked up to her, got on one knee, and she purred as I rubbed her head. Her fur was just so soft and gentle. I could keep rubbing it for hours on end…

Blake

I pushed past the people in front of me, unhappy that they were standing in my way. Didn't they know I was going to sing? And I wasn't just going to do that. I was going to rock the audience and make them think I was the best rockstar in the world.

Sweat pooled on my forehead and in my armpits. It wasn't the first time I was going to sing in front of so many people, and instead of that making me feel afraid, it energized me.

Nothing better than giving thousands of people what they came here for.

I dashed through the curtains, the roar of the crowd erupting at the same moment. I smiled, checking out the stadium. All I could see was the forest of dancing people, and the flashlights of their phones.

I was holding my electric guitar, my colleagues already positioned with their instruments. They were going to help me play the song or the collection of songs that I was going to master.

Couldn't wait until-

And ah, there it was. The crowd erupted again when the stage lights focused on me. Cocaine was one hell of a drug, and I couldn't be doing this without it.

I was addicted to it. I knew I should do something about it, but the truth of the matter was that I couldn't feel like this without first taking some hits. It's why I always felt overconfident.

Without it, intrusive thoughts started to creep into my mind, and I couldn't have that.

My fingers moving against the strings, I start to sing and shake my head, my long and blonde hair flying with me. The crowd roared again, their phones shining their flashlights.

It was dark. The moon was just above the walls of the stadium, making the place feel even more alive than it was.

And it wasn't just my fingers and head that were moving frenetically, but also my body. I couldn't stay still for a second, dashing from left to right and vice-versa, thinking about nothing but my song.

My clothes were tight. Rockstars like myself were few and far between these days, but that was okay. I had a bigger audience and more people sucking up to me than usual, I thought with a smile.

And the crowd erupted again, my ears and eyes noticing the front rows. They weren't just singing with me, but they were also chanting my name and that was a lot more than I thought I'd ever achieve in my life when I was little. Just never thought I'd have so much fame one day and that I'd be dealing so well with it.

For a moment, my eyes landed on something. Nothing more than a shadow of something that couldn't have anything to do with me, right? Wrong. The moment my eyes found it, I already froze up and couldn't focus on the song anymore.

Goddamnit, I couldn't fail now. If I looked like a fool in front of all these people, I'd lose all my sponsorships and everyone around the globe would think I was a scam.

But what I saw... It was no mistake. She was there. The woman I thought I'd marry one day.

And my eyes also noticed someone else. A man who appeared to be as young as 18 years old, standing in the middle of the crowd, too far from the front rows. I shouldn't have noticed him and yet he was now the only thought in my mind, other than my ex.

I went on, rocking and singing, shaking my head and scrubbing the strings of the guitar with my fingers. Breathing more rapidly and sweating even more than before, I was already happy the show was ending.

Couldn't get her out of my head and couldn't stop thinking about that guy. Time for the contest's result, I remembered.

I slid across the floor, sweeping my hands one last time over the strings of the guitar and closing my eyes. A huge explosion of fireworks in front of me and the crowd roared once more.

I had a rose in my mouth. Shooting up, I tossed it to the crowd and turned around. Everyone chanted my name and my band clapped, thanking me for another spectacular performance.

I walked through the curtains and into the changing room, falling into the chair. Hairdressers and other employees surrounded me, fixing me up.

"The contest's result, sir. They're here," someone said and I perked up. Ahhh, the contest, of course. I was supposed to talk to some fans after the show tonight and I thought it would be cool if we gave everyone a fair chance.

After some last makeup retouches, I made the chair whirl around and shot up, saying, "Let them in. I'm ready."

Camera men stormed into the room, ready to record the conversation I was going to have with my fans. I felt excited, but not nervous. Talking with my fans was one of the good things about being famous.

Someone opened the door and they stepped in. I froze up for a moment, realizing that one of the guys was the same I'd spotted in the crowd. Either God existed, or someone was playing a trick on me. Of all the people I could have singled out, he was one of the winners of the contest? Really?

ABDL MM SERIES AND MORE

SERIES - SWEET PACIS

1. My Caring Biker: An ABDL MM Biker Romance
2. My Loving Biker: An ABDL MM Biker Romance
3. My Protective Biker: An ABDL MM Biker Romance
4. My Obsessive Biker: An ABDL MM Biker Romance
5. My Possessive Biker: An ABDL MM Biker Romance

SERIES - NOT ENOUGH DIAPERS

1. Be my ABDL: A Gay Age Play Romance
2. Regressing the Rookie: A Gay Age Play Romance
3. Regressing the Recruit: An ABDL Romance

SERIES – REGRESSED

1. Gifting Crayons: An ABDL MM Romance
2. Sugar Mister: An ABDL MM Romance
3. Loving Little Chris: An ABDL MM Romance
4. Bedtime for Cody: An ABDL MM Romance
5. Little Crayons: An ABDL MM Romance

MM ABDL MEGA BUNDLE

Or, if you'd like, you can download this collection instead to have all of those stories together:

Fussy Littles: An ABDL MM Romance Bundle

Gay first time romances:
One Kiss Less: A Sci-Fi MM Romance
No Turning Back: A Gay Arranged Marriage Romance
Just Say Yes: An Arranged Marriage M/M Romance

Or everything in a convenient box-set:

Against All Odds: A Gay Romance Bundle

ABOUT THE AUTHORS

Jerry Hastings

Jerry Hastings is a passionate gamer, an outspoken lover of his PS4, an advocate for minority rights, and a staunch supporter of the fight against homophobia. Much more than putting words on paper, his stories change people's lives and minds.

As a writer, his specialty is gay romance. His tales are spicier and more affectionate than those usually found elsewhere. Have your soothing tea ready, because his words will make your heart beat faster than it should.

Michael Levi

Michael Levi's biggest passion? Writing steamy, romantic stories that leave his readers panting. He's currently focusing on ABDL MM romances, but his collection is diverse and there are books for everyone's tastes. If you're looking for straight to gay, first time, BBC, sissification, and more, you're going to find them on his author page.

He lives to pamper his readers, every kiss means a lot more than what meets the eye, and he loves his Alpha males. Making sure that every gay first time feels different, Michael Levi writes his stories with a cup of coffee by his side. And for inspiration, he always opens up a photo of his new crush.